Peter's Song

By Carol P. Saul
Pictures by Diane deGroat

SIMON & SCHUSTER BOOKS FOR YOUNG READERS
Published by Simon & Schuster
New York   London   Toronto   Sydney   Tokyo   Singapore

SIMON & SCHUSTER BOOKS FOR YOUNG READERS
Simon & Schuster Building, Rockefeller Center
1230 Avenue of the Americas, New York, New York 10020
Text copyright © 1992 by Carol P. Saul
Illustrations copyright © 1992 by Diane deGroat
SIMON & SCHUSTER BOOKS FOR YOUNG READERS
is a trademark of Simon & Schuster.
Designed by Vicki Kalajian
The illustrations are rendered in watercolor,
acrylic and colored pencil.
The text is set in 14 pt. Caslon 224 Book, and the
display type is Shelley Allegro Script.

Manufactured in the United States of America

10   9   8   7   6   5   4   3   2

Library of Congress Cataloging-in-Publication Data
Saul, Carol P.
Peter's song / by Carol P. Saul ;
illustrated by Diane deGroat.   p.   cm.   Summary: When
everyone in the barnyard is too busy to listen to young
Peter Pig's song, he leaves in search of a sympathetic soul,
and finds one in a friendly frog.   [1. Pigs—Fiction.
2. Frogs—Fiction.   3. Singing—Fiction.]   I. deGroat, Diane,
ill.   II. Title.   PZ7.S2504Pe   1992   [E]—dc20   91-24674   CIP

ISBN: 0-671-73812-7

To Peter, Michael and Susanna
but, most of all, to Mark

— C.S.

ne hot summer morning, Peter Pig woke up and thought of a new song.

"Hey, everybody," he said to his friends at breakfast. "I just made up a new song. Want to hear it?"

"Oh no," groaned a young sow. "Not another one of your dumb songs."

"It's not a dumb song!" said Peter. "Listen.

> *Oh, I'm a little pig,*
> *oinky oinky oinky oink,"*

"I don't want to hear your song!" squealed one of the piglets. "I want to go roll in the mud!"

"You can roll in the mud later," said Peter. "Just listen to the rest of my song."

"We don't feel like it," said the young sow. "Come on, guys, let's go." Off they went, tails in the air.

"You're no fun!" yelled Peter after them.

eter trotted around the barnyard, looking for someone who would listen to his song.

He poked his head inside the henhouse. The hens were on their perches, clucking softly to each other.

"Mrs. Speckle," said Peter. "Do you want to hear my new song? It goes like this:

Oh, I'm a little pig,
    oinky oinky oinky oink,"

"Shhh, Peter," said Mrs. Speckle. "We need complete quiet to hatch these eggs."

"I could sing it in a very tiny voice," Peter said.

The hens stared at him with their beady eyes.

"Goodbye, Peter," said Mrs. Speckle. "You have to go now."

Peter pulled his head back out of the henhouse.

"Silly old biddies," said Peter under his breath.

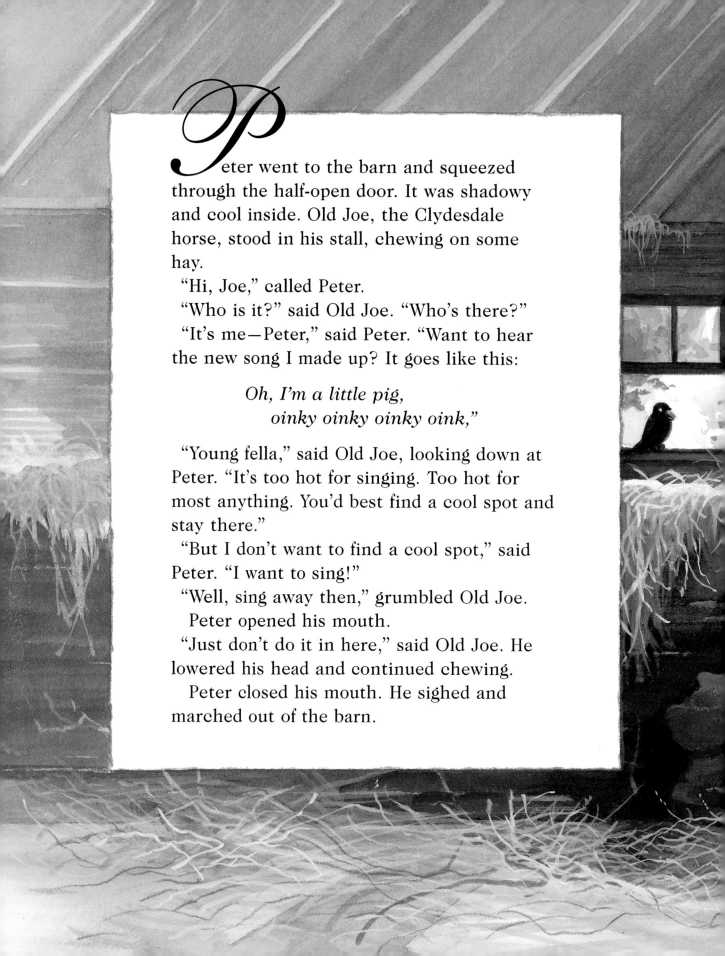

*P*eter went to the barn and squeezed through the half-open door. It was shadowy and cool inside. Old Joe, the Clydesdale horse, stood in his stall, chewing on some hay.

"Hi, Joe," called Peter.

"Who is it?" said Old Joe. "Who's there?"

"It's me—Peter," said Peter. "Want to hear the new song I made up? It goes like this:

Oh, I'm a little pig,
oinky oinky oinky oink,"

"Young fella," said Old Joe, looking down at Peter. "It's too hot for singing. Too hot for most anything. You'd best find a cool spot and stay there."

"But I don't want to find a cool spot," said Peter. "I want to sing!"

"Well, sing away then," grumbled Old Joe.

Peter opened his mouth.

"Just don't do it in here," said Old Joe. He lowered his head and continued chewing.

Peter closed his mouth. He sighed and marched out of the barn.

I know," he said to himself. "I'll go find Mrs. Bossy. She always likes to hear me sing!"

The sun was high in the sky. In the pasture, the cows stood like statues.

"Hi, Mrs. Bossy," said Peter. "I just made up a new song. Want to hear it?"

Mrs. Bossy flicked her tail. A fly buzzed away.

"Peter dear," said Mrs. Bossy. "Milking time is in a few hours. Any disturbance might make the milk go sour."

"Oh, but this is a very sweet song," said Peter. "Listen.

Oh, I'm a little pig,
oinky oinky oinky oink,"

"Not now, dear," said Mrs. Bossy. "We're not in the moooood."

*P*eter turned and started back to the farmyard, feeling very disappointed and a little hungry. When he reached the pigsty, he found all the other pigs napping in the shade.

Peter tiptoed over to his mother.

"Mom? Mom?" he whispered in her ear.

"Mmmmm," said his mother.

"Where's lunch?" said Peter.

"Lunch was over a long time ago," his mother said. She opened one eye to look at him. "Where were you?"

"I was trying to find someone who would listen to my new song," said Peter. "I went to the barn and the henhouse and every place else I could think of. And nobody wanted to listen!" There was such a big lump in Peter's throat, he could hardly speak.

"I saved you some food," said Peter's mother.

Peter saw a little pile of corncobs and carrot scrapings. He was so hungry that he ate it all in one gulp.

"Mom? Mom?" he whispered in her ear again. "Do you want to hear my song now?"

"Peter." said his mother. Her eyes were closed. "When I finish my nap, I'll be happy to listen to your song."

In a moment she was fast asleep again.

eter listened to her snore. Then he stomped out of the pigsty, feeling sadder and madder than he had ever felt in his whole life.

"That's it!" said Peter. "I'm running away!"

He marched across the farmyard and passed the barn. When he got to the big gate at the entrance to the farm, he slowed down.

He had never gone this far by himself before.

"I don't care," he told himself. "I'm leaving. And I'm not going to stop until I find somebody who will listen to my song!"

With his tail held high, Peter opened the gate and trotted down the road. He passed the next farm, and the next one, and the next.

$\mathcal{A}$fter a time, Peter came to a dusty path that led off the road. He followed it and found himself at the edge of a big pond surrounded by trees.

Birds chirped and insects buzzed. The pond was very cool, very green, and very quiet.

Peter sat at the edge of the pond and drank a little water. He looked around.

"This seems like a good place to sing," he said to himself.

He drank some more water, cleared his throat, and began to sing:

"Oh, I'm a little pig,
    oinky oinky oinky oink,
And I'm really not so big,
    oinky oinky oinky oink,
But I like to sing a song,
    oinky oinky oinky oink,
Do you want to sing along?
    oinky oinky oinky OINK!"

Peter's song echoed through the trees.
He sang the second verse a little louder:

"No one likes to hear me sing,
    oinky oinky oinky oink,
Well, they don't know anything,
    oinky oinky oinky oink,
'Cause the best part of a song,
    oinky oinky oinky oink,
Is when someone sings along,
    oinky oinky oinky OINK!"

The setting sun streamed through the
treetops. A breeze rustled the leaves. Peter
began again:

"Oh, I'm a little pig…"

"RRRibit!"

eter jumped. What was that? He sniffed the air.

"RRibit!"

Where was it coming from?

"Who said that?" asked Peter.

No one answered.

"Is anyone here?" asked Peter, a little bit louder.

SPLASH! went something in the middle of the pond. Something green leaped into the air and landed at Peter's feet.

"RRRibit!" it said.

ow!" said Peter.

The green thing sat and blinked at Peter with big, yellow eyes.

"Was that you I heard singing before?" it asked.

"Yes, that was me," said Peter.

"You have a very nice voice," said the creature. "I heard you clear across the pond."

"Gee, thanks," said Peter. "I love to sing."

"So do I," said the creature. "I'd rather sing than catch flies any day."

"Catch flies?" said Peter.

"To eat," explained the creature. "Frogs eat flies. I'm a frog."

"Ohhh," said Peter.

"My name is Francis John," said the frog. "But you can call me Frank."

"I'm a pig," said Peter. "I'm Peter. I come from a farm back there." He nodded back toward the road. "I made up a new song and nobody wanted to hear it. So I ran away."

"I see," said Frank. He blinked at Peter again. "The new song you made up—was that the song you were singing before?"

"Yes," said Peter.

"I couldn't quite hear all of it from the middle of the pond," said Frank. "Would you mind singing it again?"

"Would I mind?" cried Peter, wiggling with happiness. "I'd love to!"

"Good," said Frank. He hopped onto a rock. "I'm ready to listen now."

Peter stood up straight. He shook the mud from his tail and cleared his throat.

"*A*hem," he said.

"*Oh, I'm a little pig,*
*   oinky oinky oinky oink,*"

He sang it all the way through. He sang both verses.

"Bravo! Bravo!" said Frank.

"Thank you very much," said Peter.

Now it's my turn," said Frank.

"Okay," said Peter. He sat down to listen.

Frank hopped onto a big rock. He cleared his throat. Then he began to sing:

"I'm a frog, rribit rribit, in a pond
  (blink blink),
And there's one, rribit, thing of which I'm fond
  (blink blink),
It's to sing, rribit rribit, all the time
  (blink blink),
And make songs, rribit, which I like to rhyme
  (blink blink)."

"That was great!" said Peter, applauding.

"I liked the blinking part best."

"Thank you," said Frank.

"I know another song," said Peter.

The two new friends made music
for a long time. Peter sang songs in his sweet
high piggy voice and Frank sang in his rich
low froggy voice. They sang songs to each
other and they made up songs together.
This was their favorite:

> *"A froggie met a pig,*
>   *oinky oinky oinky oink,*
> *And they didn't dance a jig,*
>   *oinky oinky oinky oink,*
> *But together, rribit rribit, on a log*
>   *(blink blink)*
> *They sang, oinky, rribit, piggie*
>   *and the frog*
>   *(blink blink)."*

When the moon rose over the pond, bathing it in silver light, Peter looked up in surprise.

"It's late," he said. "I have to go home now."

"Ohh, don't go!" said Frank. "We were having such a good time."

"I know," said Peter. "But my mother will be so worried about me." He turned to go, then stopped. "I could come back another day."

"Good," said Frank. "Come back tomorrow. Late afternoon is the best time. We can sing together some more."

"Okay," said Peter. "Will you be here?"

"Definitely," said Frank. "Every evening until the weather turns cold."

"Then I'll see you tomorrow," said Peter. "Goodbye!"

"See you tomorrow," answered Frank.

$\mathcal{P}$eter raced up the road that would lead him back to the farm. As he headed toward home, he sang softly to himself:

"'Cause the best part of a song,
 oinky oinky oinky oink,
Is when someone sings along,
 oinky oinky oinky oink!"